The
Aqua
Adventure

Written By
Michael Azmy

"The Aqua Adventure" published through Young Author Academy.

Young Author Academy FZCO

Dubai, United Arab Emirates

www.youngauthoracademy.com

ISBN: 9798847182119

Printed by Amazon Direct Publishing.

Dedicated to my mom.

I am so lucky to have such a

heart-warming and dedicated mom.

She pushes me and pushes me until I achieve

what I really want to achieve.

Not only happiness but love fills her heart.

Contents

- Chapter One -

I am Michael

Hi! I am Michael!

I am an ordinary kid.

I mean… sure I do ordinary things. I like ordinary things.

But there is one thing that makes me unique.

To many, I am…

… ADVENTUROUS!

For example, when I was two years old,

I jumped into a lion cage and I did not even cry.

And when I was five years old, I was literally playing

with snakes and was not even afraid of them!

At school one day, I was feeling really nervous. On this particular day, I was expecting to get my math test results. This was a test that was important because it was going to be used to help me get into my next school.

Normally, my maths test results were not so good but throughout the past couple of months, I had persevered severely with my school work. The teacher slowly handed me my paper. My heart was racing. As I slowly lifted my hand to take my test paper from her, I could hear my teacher handing the other papers out to the other students and let's just say, the majority of the kids weren't so lucky. There were some groans and gasps. This just made me more and more nervous about my own result.

Millimeter by millimeter, my hand moved to reveal my score that was written at the top of my paper. I had passed! Well and truly passed…

I got an 82% - enough to to get through.

For the rest of the school day, I just watched the clock… Ring! The end of the day had come so I darted home to my parents to inform them of the terrific news.

- Chapter Two -

An Ocean Sail

It turned out to be the best day of my life because my mom promised we would go for a trip on a boat because of my excellent maths paper result. How could this day get any better? This was the first time since my seventh birthday that I had been on a boat.

I remember when I was seven years old, my mom and dad hired a boat and we took some of my closest school friends on a cruise. We had an amazing time on the boat sailing on the crystal clear waters of the ocean.

Days passed until the day we were going to take the boat for a sail on the ocean. There I was, in the car looking out of the window gazing at the amiable beach. I was so excited.

I bolted over to the monumental boat and rapidly realized that the TV in the boat was showing one of my favorite series, Merlin. This trip on the boat was going to be awesome!

After a couple of hours of just sitting and relaxing, sailing on the ocean, I was anxious to enjoy my time from the top deck of the boat. I sat there with the gentle breeze on my face as I watched the sun start to descend towards the horizon.

After a while, my parents joined me and they suggested that we jump in the water for a refreshing swim. I was so fascinated by this tremendous idea so I leaped into the azure waters of the beautiful ocean.

After I hit the water, a swirling, bizarre tornado of water abruptly formed and hooked me in. I was taken through the whirlpool of water. I couldn't retreat back to the surface of the water. What lie in front of me was nothing that I could have ever expected…

- Chapter Three -

Discovering Magic

…As I swam throughout the waters, I noticed a sign in the sea of blue….   "No trespassing!"

I knew what I had to do…

I waited for the perfect moment and hastily rushed towards the sign.

Hundreds of questions zoomed around my head like,

'Where was I?' And,

'Do my parents know where I went?'

As I swam through the depths of the ocean, I noticed a huge city in the distance.

I swam closely to the city and noticed jovial kids playing in a park; an underwater park on the seabed of the ocean. What on earth had I come across?

Fish with different hues dazzled and swayed. Archaic, rusted walls stood gracefully. Most importantly, joy filled the place.

Fish swum around me and for some reason, I could breathe well under the water. The majestic city shone in the background. I swam closer and closer to this mystery site.

The smell of delicious food wafted by my nose. I was dumbfounded as to what on earth this place was, so I asked one of the strangers that I came across where on earth I was.

Suddenly, a group of majestic people approached me. One of the men just barked at me, "It's none of your business boy! How did you get here?"

His threats were interrupted when an elegant woman approached and firmly said to the men. "How dare you welcome a guest in this manner, you atrocious barbarian!

Let him go!"

Then she turned to me and said in a quiet voice, "Are you okay sweety? Come, I will get you some food. I will also have my staff show you to your own room. You are welcome in our Kingdom."

I came to the conclusion that the elegant woman was the man's wife, because he was dressed in royal attire and she was also dressed in elegant Queen-looking, royal, regal attire; a perfect match for a brawny, broad man.

After enjoying a beautiful meal prepared by the royal staff, I went to take a swim along the hectic roads of this *Aqualand*. I came across a sheet of paper stuck to a wall, reading, *"Join the Race."*

As I read more of the rules, I learned that the race objective was to find five valuable gold coins.

'Who will find the most?' It read.

The poster on the wall continued to explain that the Great Race was a tradition that had been held for thousands of years in this magical underwater city.

I was wondering if I should participate in the race or not.

After a while of thinking, I knew I had to. This was a great opportunity to prove that I was worthy of being there, and I could possibly stand out from the rest, even if they had been prepared since the day they were born for such a challenge. Whilst I had found myself here, I thought, 'Why not?'

I did wonder about my parents and if they were worried about me, but I also had wandered into a pretty amazing place, almost a fictional place. I had wondered seriously if I was dreaming. Perhaps I was? I also didn't know how to leave the magical place under the water. I didn't know how to get back through the vortex of water that thrust me deep into the water in the first place.

I darted to a colossal building where I needed to register for the race. I wanted to win that prize of five glamorous coins. Apparently, winning five golden coins would have the winner win a wish that was to be granted by the King and Queen and 10,000 Gallings, which was the currency of this Aqua land. I hastily signed up for it.

Later, as I was in my bed trying to sleep I just couldn't stop thinking, 'Who would win? Could I actually win?'

- Chapter Four -

The Great Race

I woke up at 6:00 am on the morning of the Great Race and swiftly bolted to the building. To my surprise, the referee of the race started to call out the instructions. "Every body! The rules are simple! No punching. No kicking. No biting. Look out for things! You never know, there might be something waiting to strike."

I was nervous and anxious. I started off slow but later on, I picked up my pace. Surely but slowly, I started to speed up with my swimming and searching so that I could find more places that would be good hiding spots for miniature coins. Suddenly everyone started whispering and making a fuss, and soon I realized that one of the boys had found one of the five coins. This just made me more and more nervous.

As a result, my speed went straight back to zero and I sensed everything was going to be worse. But I was wrong, very wrong because the moment I had that thought …

…I found a coin!

I was so elated and relieved.

This brought my speed booming to what felt like the speed of light confidently! When I thought nothing could be going better…I found *another* coin hiding under one of the rocks.

I swam around in happiness. Dancing around while my fellow competitors' eyes filled with envy. Not only shame, but fear covered their goosebumps. They indignantly marched along with massive frowns on their face. Jealousy spread the underwater land.

Hours later after an arduous journey, my energy was still high and I was swimming and marching around elatedly, but then the worst news that could ever happen…

...HAPPENED!!!!!!

The same boy from earlier found another coin. That left us in a tie breaker. It was now or never!

Who would find the last coin?

Or would either of us?

In the distance I found the boy who had found two coins. I looked at him and then I looked forward. Out of the blue we both saw a glimmer, a miniature shining object on the bottom of the ocean bed. We both scrambled to reach it.

I dived deep and luckily just managed to grab it in the nick of time. I was so relieved, I won! I could hear the crowds around me cheering my name but I was still feeling really dejected. I was now missing my parents even more. I didn't have anyone to celebrate the win with.

- Chapter Five -

A Wish Come True

For winning, the King actually did grant me a wish! I wished to be free, to return to where I truly belonged.

In a split-second, after revealing my deepest wish to the King that I wanted to return to my parents, I was whisked back up from the deepest part of the beautiful under water city back up to the surface of the ocean.

The first thing I heard as I sped back through the ocean vortex was ear-splitting sirens and the voice of my mom weeping and calling my name. I rushed to her in excitement while she welcomed me in her arms.

About the Author

Michael Azmy

Michael is a nine year old Dubai based young author with a flair for fabulously imaginative stories. At school, Michael loves P.E. and Sports and in his spare time, he loves to play football, and he loves to climb.

To make the world a better place, Michael would help with preventing world hunger and help those less fortunate.

Follow Michael's publishing journey here,

www.youngauthoracademy.com/michael-azmy

SCAN ME

(with your camera phone)

Printed in Great Britain
by Amazon